D1015845

MINI CLASSICS

THE
UGLY
DUCKLING

A Parragon Book

Published by
Parragon Books,
Unit 13-17, Avonbridge Trading Estate,
Atlantic Road, Avonmouth, Bristol BS11 9QD.

Produced by
The Templar Company plc,
Pippbrook Mill, London Road, Dorking, Surrey RH4 1JE.

Copyright © 1994 Parragon Book Service Limited

Designed by Mark Kingsley-Monks

Printed and bound in Great Britain

ISBN 1-85813-680-6

MINI CLASSICS

THE
UGLY DUCKLING

RETOLD BY STEPHANIE LASLETT
ILLUSTRATED BY ANDREW GEESON

It was summer, and the countryside looked beautiful. The wheat was yellow, the oats were green, and down by the canal grew a forest of tall dock leaves.

Here a duck had built herself a warm nest, and now proudly sat on her six pretty eggs. Five of them were white, but the sixth,

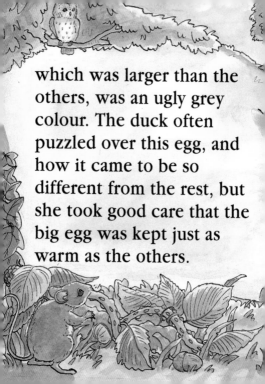

which was larger than the others, was an ugly grey colour. The duck often puzzled over this egg, and how it came to be so different from the rest, but she took good care that the big egg was kept just as warm as the others.

This was her first set of eggs and she was very pleased with herself. She had looked at the eggs at least a hundred and fifty times, when, to her joy, she saw a

tiny crack on two of them,
and by midday two little
yellow heads were poking
out from the shells. Soon the
five white eggs were empty.

Ten pairs of beady little eyes gazed out upon the green world.

Day after day passed, but the big egg still showed no sign of cracking, and the mother duck grew more and more impatient.

"I can't think what is the matter with it," she grumbled to her neighbour.

"Let me look at it," said the old duck. "Ah, I thought so; it is a turkey's egg. Once, when I was young, I was tricked into sitting on a brood of turkey's eggs myself, and when they hatched the creatures were so stupid that nothing would make them learn to swim."

"Well, I will give it a little longer," sighed the duck. "If it does not come out of its shell in another twenty-four hours, I will just leave it alone and teach the rest of them to swim properly and to find their own food. I really can't be expected to do two things at once." And with a fluff of her feathers she pushed the egg into the middle of the nest and settled down.

The duck sat all through the next day and, by the evening, she thought she saw a tiny crack in the upper part of the shell. Tha night she could hardly slee for excitement and, when she woke with the first

treaks of light, she felt
something stirring under
her. Yes, here it was at last;
and as she moved, an
awkward big duckling
tumbled headlong out of
the last remaining shell.

And he was ugly! Even his
poor mother had to admit
it, though she only said he
was "large" and "strong."

She was surprised to see
her new youngster was
covered in dull brown fluff
and had a long skinny neck.

"You will learn to swim
quickly," she said, and
indeed he did, for he loved
the water and paddled along
with all his might. But he
was not half as pretty as
the little yellow balls that

followed the mother duck.
When they returned they
found their neighbour
watching from the bank.

"No, he is certainly not a
young turkey," she whispered
to the mother, "for even
though he is lean and skinny,
there is something rather
unusual about him, and he
holds his head up well."

"It is very kind of you to say so," answered the mother, who by this time had some secret doubts about his loveliness.

"He is different, somehow from the others, but one cannot expect all one's children to be beautiful!"

By this time the ducks had reached the centre of

the yard. There sat the farm's oldest duck and she was treated with great respect by all the fowls who lived there.

"You must go up and bow low before her," whispered the mother to her children, nodding her head in the direction of the old lady, "and keep your legs well apart, as you see me do. No well-bred duckling turns in his toes."

The little ducks tried hard to make their small fat bodies copy the movements of their mother, and the old lady was quite pleased with them; but the rest of the ducks smirked, and said to one another:

"Oh, dear me, not more ducklings! The yard is full already." Then one of them spotted the ugly duckling.

"Did you ever see anything quite as ugly as that great tall creature? He is a disgrace to any brood. I shall go and chase him out!" She fluffed up her feathers, ran over to the poor ugly duckling and pecked him on the neck.

It was the first time the duckling had felt any pain and he gave a loud quack.

Quickly his mother turned to protect him.

"Leave him alone," she said fiercely, "or I will send for his father. He was not troubling you."

"No; but he is so ugly and awkward that we don't want him here," answered the other duck. And though the duckling did not understand the meaning of the words, he felt he was being blamed, and became more uncomfortable still when the old duck who ruled the farmyard spoke out:

"It certainly is a great pity he is so different from these other beautiful darlings. If only he could be hatched all over again!"

The poor little fellow drooped his head, and did not know where to look, but he was comforted when his mother answered

"He may not be quite as handsome as the others, but he swims better, and is very strong. I am sure he will make his way in the world as well as anybody."

"Well, you must all make yourselves at home," said the old duck as she waddled off. And so they did, all except the ugly duckling, who was snapped at by everyone when they thought his mother was not looking. Even the huge turkey never passed by without making fun of him.

Soon his brothers and sisters, who would not have noticed any difference unless it had been pointed out to them, became as rude and unkind to him as all the rest.

At last the ugly duckling could bear it no longer.

"Tonight I shall run away!" he decided.

So when the ducks and hens were still asleep, he crept out through an open door, and under cover of the dock leaves scrambled along

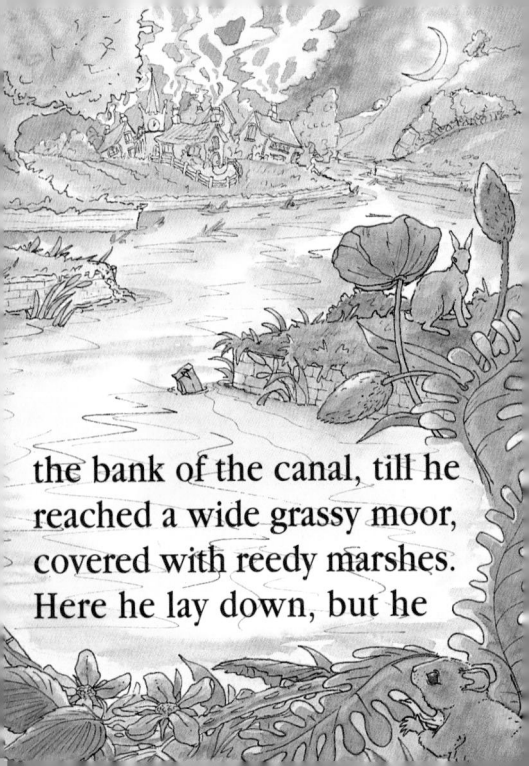

the bank of the canal, till he
reached a wide grassy moor,
covered with reedy marshes.
Here he lay down, but he

was too tired and too frightened to fall asleep.

He stayed awake until the sun came up. Then the reeds began to rustle and he saw that he was surrounded by wild ducks. The poor duckling was too tired to run away again so he stood up and bowed politely. The wild ducks just stared at him.

"You are ugly," they said; "but I suppose it is no business of ours, unless you wish to marry one of our daughters, and that we should not allow." And the duckling answered that he had no idea of marrying anybody, and only wanted to be left alone after his long journey.

So for two whole days he lay quietly among the reeds, eating whatever food he could find, and drinking the water of the moorland pool, till he felt quite strong again.

"I am happy here," he sighed; "I feel safe away from everyone, with nobody to bite me and tell me how ugly I am."

He was thinking these thoughts, when two young geese caught sight of him as they were having their evening splash among the reeds, looking for their supper.

"Hello," they said. "We are getting tired of this moor and we are off to find another, where the lakes are larger and the food is better. Would you like to come with us?"

"Is it nicer than this?" asked the duckling, doubtfully. But the words were hardly out of his mouth when "Bang! Bang!" and the two geese fell dead beside him.

At the sound of the gun the wild ducks in the rushes flew into the air, and then more shots rang out. "Bang! Bang!"

Luckily for him, the duckling could not fly, and he floundered through the water till he could hide himself amongst some tall ferns which grew in a hollow. But just when he thought he was safe, he suddenly came face to face with a huge creature on four legs. It was a dog!

The fierce animal stood and gazed at him with a long red tongue hanging out of his mouth. The duckling grew cold with terror, and tried to hide his head beneath his little wings.

"It's all over!" he moaned, but the dog just sniffed at him and splashed on through the water.

"Well, let me be thankful!" the duckling said to himself. "I am too ugly even for a dog to eat." And he curled himself up in the soft grass till the shots died away in the distance.

When all had been quiet for a long time, and there were only the stars to see him, he crept out and looked around. Vowing never to go near a pool again, he marched off across the moor in the opposite direction. After a time, he came to a small, tumbledown cottage. The door hung on ust one hinge, and through the gap the duckling could see a plain little room lit by a tiny fire. It seemed warm and safe so nervously he edged inside, and lay down under a chair close to the broken door, so that he could escape if necessary. But no-one seemed to see him or smell him; so he spent the rest of the night in peace.

Now in the cottage dwelt an old woman with her cat and her hen; and it was

really they, and not she, who
were masters of the house.
The old woman loved them
both as if they were her own
children, and never argued

with them. If the duckling wished to stay in the house, he would have to ask permission from the cat and the hen. When it grew light

next morning, the cat and
the hen noticed their visitor.

He stood trembling before them, with his eye on the door ready to escape at any moment. But the cat and the hen did not seem too fierce, and the duckling became less afraid as they came near.

"Can you lay eggs?" asked the hen. The duckling answered meekly:

"No; I don't know how."

Disgusted, the hen turned her back, and then the cat came forward.

"Can you ruffle your fur when you are angry, or purr when you are pleased?" she asked. And again the duckling had to admit that he could do nothing but swim, which did not seem to be of much use to anybody.

So the cat and the hen went straight off to the old woman, who was still in bed. "We have found such a useless creature here," they said. "He calls himself a duckling; but he can neither lay eggs nor purr! What should we do with him?"

"Why, we must keep him!" replied the old woman

briskly. "I am sure he will learn to lay eggs. Let him stay here for a bit, and see what happens." And so the duckling stayed for three weeks, but nothing in the way of eggs happened at all. Then the sun came out, and the air grew warm, and the duckling longed for a swim.

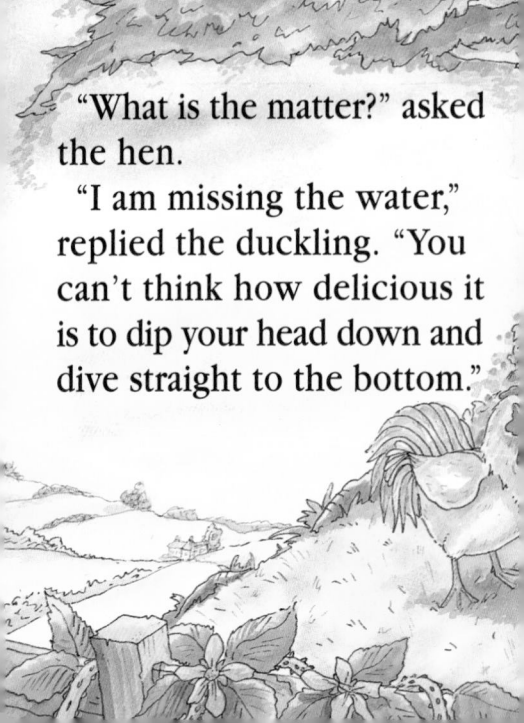

"What is the matter?" asked the hen.

"I am missing the water," replied the duckling. "You can't think how delicious it is to dip your head down and dive straight to the bottom."

"I don't think I should enjoy it," replied the hen, doubtfully. "And I don't think the cat would like it either." And the cat agreed there was nothing he would hate so much as a swim.

"I must get to the water,"
repeated the duck. And the
cat and the hen, who felt
hurt that he should want to
leave them, answered
shortly:

"Very well then, go."

The duckling was a polite little fellow and would have liked to say goodbye, and thank them for their kindness; but they had both turned their backs on him, so he went out of the rickety door feeling rather sad. But as soon as he was splashing about in the water once more he forgot his troubles.

He even managed to ignore the rude looks he got from creatures passing him.

For a while he was quite content; but then the weather began to change, and everything grew very wet and uncomfortable. The duckling soon found that it is one thing to enjoy being wet in the water, and quite

another to like being damp
on land. Time passed and
the duckling was bewildered
to find the river getting
hard and slippery! Winter
was coming and the water
was icing over.

One day, as the sun was
setting like a great scarlet
globe, the duckling heard
the sound of whirring wings,

and there, flying high in the sky, was a flock of swans. They were as white as the snow which had fallen during the night, and their long yellow-billed necks stretched southwards.

They were not exactly sure where they were heading, but they knew they would reach a land where the sun shone all day. The duckling was spellbound. He had never seen anything so beautiful in all his life.

"Oh, if only I could go with them!" he sighed. But, of course, that was not possible; and besides, what would those beautiful beings want with an ugly companion like him?

Sadly, he walked down to a sheltered pool and dived to the very bottom, and tried to think it was the greatest happiness he could dream of. But it was no good; he couldn't pretend!

Every morning it grew
colder, and the duckling had
to work hard to keep himself
warm. Soon the day came
when he never warmed up

at all but shivered from
dawn until dusk. At last,
after one bitter night on the
river, the duckling's legs
moved so slowly that the ice

crept closer and closer, and when the morning light broke he was caught as fast as if he was in a trap. Stiff and numb with cold, he toppled over and lay stretched out on the ice.

A few hours more and the poor duckling's life would have ended. But, by good fortune, a man was crossing the river on his way to work, and straightaway saw what had happened. He stamped on the ice with his thick wooden clogs until it broke. Then the man picked up the duckling and tucked him under his sheepskin coat until his frozen bones began to thaw a little.

Instead of going to work, the man turned back and took the duckling home to his children. They gave him warm food to eat and put him in a box by the fire, and when they came back from school he was much more comfortable. They were kind little children, and wanted to play with him;

but, alas! the poor fellow had never played in his life, and thought they wanted to tease him.

He flew straight into the milk-pan, and then into the butter-dish, and from that into the grain-barrel, and at last, terrified by the noise and confusion, he scuttled right out of the door, and hid himself in the snow amongst the bushes at the back of the house.

In later years he could never remember exactly how he had spent the rest of the winter. He only knew that he was very miserable

nd that he never had
nough to eat. But by-and-
y things grew better. The
arth became softer, the
un hotter, the birds sang,
nd the flowers once more
ppeared in the grass.

As the days passed, he
egan to feel different. His
ody seemed larger, and his
wings stronger. Slowly he

stretched them out and
beat them up and down.
Then, to his astonishment,
he saw that he had left the
ground far below and was
flying through the air!

Oh, how glorious it felt to be rushing like the wind, wheeling first one way and then the other! He had never thought that flying could be like that. Away on a hillside he could see an apple orchard full of pink blossom. As he flew closer he saw a cottage by the banks of the canal. He anded gracefully on the ground and looked about him. There, walking slowly past the apple trees, was a flock of the same beautiful birds he had seen so many months ago. Fascinated, he watched them one by one step into the canal, and float quietly upon the water as if it was part of them.

"I will follow them," said the duckling to himself. "Ugly though I am, I would rather be killed by them than suffer all I have suffered from cold and hunger, and from the ducks and birds who have mistreated me so badly."

Quickly, he swam after them as fast as he could.

It did not take him long to reach the birds, for they had stopped to rest in a green pool shaded by a tree whose branches swept the water.

When they saw him coming
towards them, some of the
younger ones swam out to
meet him with cries of
welcome.

The poor duckling could not understand why. Trembling, he turned to one of the older birds, and said:

"If I am to die, I would rather you should kill me. I don't know why I was ever hatched, for I am too ugly to live." And as he spoke, he bowed his head and looked down into the water.

Reflected in the still pool he saw many white shapes, with long necks and golden bills, and then he searched for his own dull grey body and awkward skinny neck.

But no such thing was there.
Instead, he beheld beneath
him a beautiful white swan!

Some children ran from the cottage with biscuit and cake to feed the swans.

"The new one is the best of all," they said. "His feathers are whiter and his beak more golden than the rest."

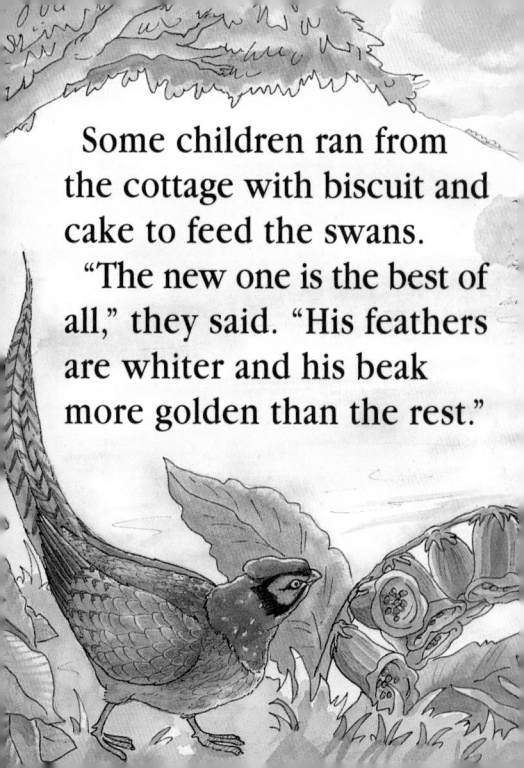

And when he heard that, the duckling thought he might cry with happiness. He remembered how everyone had teased him and how lonely and miserable he had been.

"But now all my suffering is over," he thought. "At last I know what it is to be truly happy!"

HANS CHRISTIAN ANDERSEN

Hans Christian Andersen was born in
Odense, Denmark, on April 2nd, 1805.
His family was very poor and throughout his
life he suffered much unhappiness. Even
after he had found success as a writer,
Andersen felt something of an outsider, an
aspect which often emerged in his stories,
such as here in *The Ugly Duckling*, one of
his best-loved tales.
His fairy stories, famous throughout the
world, include *The Snow Queen*,
The Little Mermaid and *The Emperor's New
Clothes*, and are amongst the most
frequently translated works of literature.
He died in 1875.